this
·little·orchard·
book belongs to

....

....

ORCHARD BOOKS
96 Leonard Street, London EC2A 4RH
Orchard Books Australia
14 Mars Road, Lane Cove, NSW 2066
1 86039 537 6 (hardback)
1 86039 490 6 (paperback)
First published in Great Britain in 1997
Copyright © Nicola Smee 1997
The right of Nicola Smee to be identified as the author and illustrator of this work has been
asserted by her in accordance with the Copyright, Designs and Patents Act, 1988.
A CIP catalogue record for this book is available from the British Library.
Printed in Italy

Freddie visits the doctor

Nicola Smee

• little • orchard •

I've got a sore throat
and so has Bear.
Mum's taking us to
see the Doctor.

"Open wide
and say, Aaah!"
says Doctor.

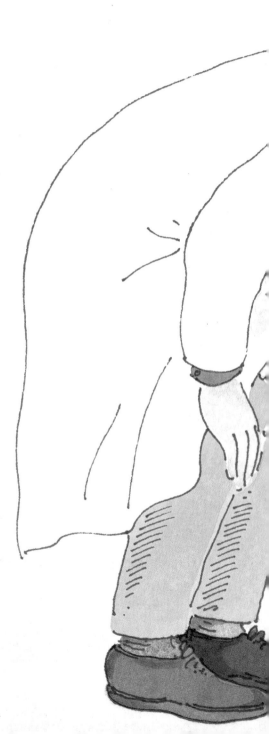

He looks into
our ears with
a little torch.

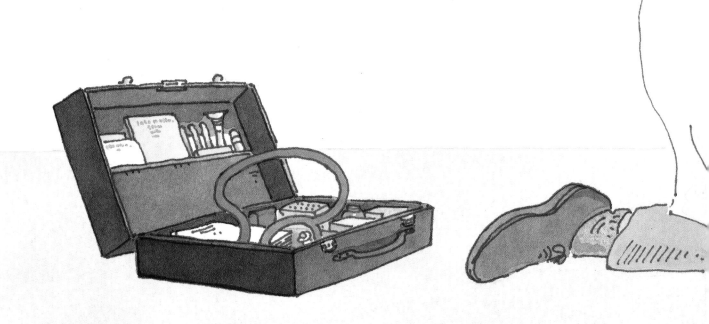

"Take a deep breath," says Doctor, and he listens to our chests with his stethoscope.

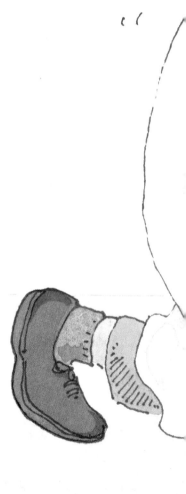

"Bear's fine, but this medicine will soon make you better, Freddie," says Doctor.

"Here you are, Freddie," says the chemist.

"Time for your medicine," says Mum. "You'll soon be well again."

Mmmm, that's nice!
My throat feels
better already.